DEADSTOCK

STONEBUNNY PRESS

This is a work of fiction. Names, characters, places and incidents either are the product of the author's imagination or are used fictitiously. Any resemblance to actual persons, living or dead, or to events and locales is entirely coincidental.

DEADSTOCK

First Edition, 2011

Copyright © 2011 Ian Rogers

Published by Stonebunny Press

195 Drew Street, Oshawa, ON L1H 5A4, Canada

Book design by Melanie Fischer

Cover elements, 'Revolver' © Jean Scheijen;

'Fire Flames' © Patricia Ruiz Diaz;

'Sunset in Oklahoma' © krazykaty http://www.sxc.hu/profile/krazykaty.

Title page elements, 'Stained Edge' © Billy Alexander; 'Evil Skull' © Petr Kovar

Author photo © Kathryn Verhulst-Rogers

All rights reserved. No part of this book may be reproduced or transmitted in any form or by any means, electronic or mechanical, including photocopying, recording or by any information storage and retrieval system, without the prior written permission of the copyright holder and publisher, except for the inclusion of brief quotations in a review.

Visit our website at

www.stonebunnypress.ca

ISBN: 978-0-9868547-1-2

10 9 8 7 6 5 4 3 2 1

Published in Canada

DEADSTOCK

IAN ROGERS

To Woodrow,
Horror Trails!

This one is for Scott Craig.

1

THEY rode at night because it was cooler. Navigating by compass and the stars, they reached the Nevada border, and Raisy began asking the question. *Is this the town? Is it this one?* Dryden tried to keep his temper, but eventually he stopped answering her. They didn't speak for the rest of the trip. August Finch broke the silence every now and again, hissing and growling from the oversized saddlebag that lay across the back of Raisy's percheron.

As the sky started to brighten, they could see the silhouettes of buildings rising on the far horizon. Raisy clucked her horse into a trot and went looking for the signpost that would tell them the name of the town. A few minutes later, she came back smiling.

"Thank God," she said. "We're finally here."

"This is it?" Dryden asked. "Ashes?"

"That's what the sign says." Raisy looked over her shoulder at the darkly brooding town. "What the hell kind of name is that, anyway?"

"This is hard country. The people who settled out here gave their towns hard names to go with it."

Raisy nodded, recalling some of the other towns they had passed through — Rattlesnake, Poison Ridge, Burning Hills.

"It doesn't matter to us," Dryden went on. "Chester doesn't live in the town proper. He's on the outskirts."

Raisy swung her mount around in a circle and looked out across the desert. The sun was slowly giving the land back its color — the bleach-white hardpan, the burnt-orange rocks, the savage green sagebrush.

"We're on the outskirts," she said.

"On the other side," Dryden said patiently.

Raisy flicked the brim of her hat. "Figures."

The bundle in her saddlebag let out a low yowl.

Dryden sighed and gigged his horse forward.

The town came into clearer focus as they drew closer. The squat shapes resolved themselves into two lines of buildings divided by a wide dust-choked main street. The sun poured over everything in a molten glaze and made it look like they were riding into the middle of hell itself.

"Dryden."

Raisy's curt tone got his attention. He turned and followed her gaze to a dust cloud rising in the distance on their left side. They heard the echoing clomp of hooves and pulled up to wait. August Finch hissed loudly and Dryden told him to hobble his lip. A strong breeze pulled the dust cloud away and they saw a rider coming toward them. He was dressed all in black, from his work shirt to his jeans to the flat-crowned hat on his head. There was a tin star on his shirt and a pistol on his hip. The sunlight glinted off both. He drew up alongside them, a silver-haired man in his sixties with deep furrows down in his cheeks and wavy ones that ran across his brow like worry lines.

"Top o' the morning," he said in a dry, cracked voice. He turned to Raisy and tapped his hat with a crooked finger. "Miss."

Dryden eyes flicked briefly to Raisy, but she nodded neutrally to the rider. She preferred "Miss" to "Ma'am," but not by much, and you could never tell what was going to set her off.

"You heading into town?" the rider asked, turning his attention back to Dryden.

"Just passing through, Marshal."

The rider looked down at the tin star on his shirt and grinned sheepishly. "Oh," he said, embarrassed. "Forgive my manners. I'm Tad Jacobs."

Dryden nodded. "Name's Sam Dryden. This is Raisy."

"Just Raisy?" Jacobs cocked an eyebrow at her.

"Just Raisy," she agreed.

"A pleasure," Jacobs said. "Before I can officially welcome you to town, I'm afraid I'll have to ask if you folks is heeled." He saw their perplexed expressions and raised his hands in a placatory gesture. "I just need to check 'em. I don't need to confiscate 'em."

"Check 'em for what, Marshal?" Dryden asked.

"Had some trouble here lately," the marshal said obscurely. "Just want to keep things safe."

Dryden looked over at Raisy, saw the fiery look in her eyes, and gave her a stern look. *Keep cool, Raisy. Just keep cool.*

"That's fine, Marshal," Dryden said. "We ain't got much to declare, anyway."

He opened his duster and withdrew an ancient-looking six-shooter from a cracked-leather holster. He spun it around and passed it butt-first to the marshal.

Jacobs took the gun and held it in both hands, staring at it like he'd never seen one like it before. His bushy eyebrows went up a notch. "This real?" he asked skeptically.

Dryden nodded.

Ian Rogers

Jacobs continued to scrutinize the gun. The grip was made of green wood, which was strange in itself, but the number 14 had been burned into the grain on one side, and that was even stranger. He opened the chamber and looked inside. Empty. He gave Dryden a questioning look.

"It's an antique my daddy left me," Dryden said. "It don't shoot right, but I like to keep it close, just the same."

Jacobs spun the barrel, snapped it shut with a flick of his wrist, and handed it back. He nudged his horse over to Raisy who had unbuttoned her long black frock coat and was now holding it open for the marshal's inspection. Jacobs took one look inside and recoiled backward, almost falling off his mount.

"Mercy!" he said, and uttered a shaky laugh. "What's a pretty girl need with so many knives?"

Raisy closed her coat and refastened the buttons. "Why, Marshal," she said in an overly sweet tone that made Dryden wince. "I think you just answered your own question."

Jacobs looked over at Dryden, who shrugged as if to say *Women, who can understand them?*

Raisy slapped a black lacquered case strapped to the back of her saddle. "I got some more in here. You want to see them?"

Jacobs tipped his hat. "That's okay, Miss." He looked over at Dryden. "So, you said you folks was just passing through?"

"We're on our way to the Groom ranch," Dryden said. "I'm told it's on the other side of town."

Jacobs tilted his hat back and scratched his forehead. "Yeah, that's about right. You go out to the far end of the main street and you'll come to the drop. It's pretty steep, but you can make it if you're careful. From the bottom it's about an hour's ride to the Groom place."

Dryden picked up his reins. "Much obliged, Marshal."

Jacobs seemed to hesitate for a moment, then said: "I hear Chester's been having some trouble with his cattle lately."

"That's the rumor."

"You here to help him out?"

Dryden noticed the marshal's wondering gaze moving back and forth between him and Raisy. It was hard to tell if Jacobs was fishing for information or if he was just taken aback by what a strange pair they made. Dryden with his babyface looks and haunted blue eyes; Raisy with her flaming red hair and a mouth that got them into trouble on a regular basis. Throw in his greenwood gun and Raisy's penchant for blades, and it wasn't a surprise that they drew a certain amount of attention. Usually the wrong kind.

Dryden said, "We're here to do whatever we can."

"You both friends of Chester's?" Jacobs asked.

"He and my daddy fought together in the Long Plains War," Dryden said.

"Good of you to come out, then. Chester thinks it's rustlers after his cattle, but…" Jacobs shook his head.

"What do you think it is, Marshal?" Raisy asked.

"Well," Jacobs said, "Ashes is the only town around for fifty miles. If someone here was messing with Chester's cattle, or anyone else's, people would know about it. I've been out to his place three times in the past month and I ain't seen hide nor hair of anyone. Not rustlers, not banditos, not no one."

"Things aren't always as they appear," Dryden said.

"Ain't that the truth," Jacobs said. "The God's honest." A look of unease suddenly crept onto his face like a cloud crossing in front of the sun. "I seen one of his cattle," he said in a low voice. "Afterwards."

"Yes?" Dryden prompted him.

Ian Rogers

Jacobs swallowed dryly and shook his head. He turned his horse toward town and called back over his shoulder.

"You'll see."

2

DRYDEN and Raisy rode through town without stopping. They glanced at the few struggling businesses: a saloon called The Old Bat; a boarding house called the Sleep E-Z; a general store; a smithy; a barbershop; a livery stable. The buildings seemed to blend together into one long, dusty, wind-scoured, sun-bleached façade.

"What did you make of that marshal in black?" Dryden asked conversationally.

"I ain't decided," Raisy replied. "Couldn't tell if he was dim or just playing the part. You got to have some brains in your head to be a marshal. Or at least that's what I heard. So I'm leaning toward the latter."

"But why would he act that way?" Dryden asked, as much to himself as to Raisy.

"That's the question." Raisy was silent a moment. "You ever heard of a marshal asking to see what you're packing and they don't confiscate it?"

"Nope. Why do you think he wanted to see our weapons?"

Raisy was quiet for so long that Dryden didn't think she was going to answer him. Then she finally said, "It's like he was waiting for us."

"For us? As in you and me specifically?"

Raisy grunted.

"Our faces might not be known, but our weapons stand out some."

Dryden nodded. "Nice to know our reputation precedes us."

"Yeah," Raisy said, "but what do the marshals want with us?"

Dryden didn't have an answer for that, and Raisy didn't seem to have one either.

They rode on in silence.

3

ON the far side of town, the main street sloped abruptly in a series of plateaus that looked like the steps of a giant staircase. At the bottom the land spread out like an enormous plate glimmering under the naked sun.

Dryden and Raisy clucked their horses forward and moved slowly along the steep path. At a couple of points they had to climb down to walk their horses across washouts, but a few of hours later they reached the bottom. Dryden figured it was already a hundred degrees and liable to get hotter as the day crawled sluggishly toward noon. There was no humidity and his mouth was dry as dust. He didn't understand why anyone would want to settle in such a godforsaken place.

Down here at the bottom of the drop he noticed the ground was actually one enormous jigsaw puzzle of cracks and fissures. The horses kicked up clouds of aromatic dust that hung in the air behind them as if frozen in time.

"It's alkali," Raisy said, wrinkling her nose. "This all used to be a lake."

An hour later they came to a signpost sticking out of the ground. In letters almost too faded to read were the words NO

Ian Rogers

TRESPASSING. Through a shimmer heat haze, they could see a wooden gate up ahead, and the long skeletal expanse of a corral packed full of cattle. They could hear the animals stomping their hooves and bawling moodily.

As they rode closer, the rest of the ranch came into view. There was a small, squat house that looked as if it had survived its share of windstorms. The barn that looked like it had been painted red about a thousand years ago and was now a listless maroon. There was also a water pump, a work shed, and the tumbledown remains of what had once been a smokehouse.

Dryden and Raisy rode into the wide, dusty yard and dismounted. At the left side of the house, two girls in blue sundresses were tending a patch of corn and watching them with wide, wary eyes. Another girl, this one younger than the other two, was sitting on the ground in front of the porch. She was playing with something, and as Dryden and Raisy came closer, they saw it was a scorpion.

"Careful there, peanut," Dryden said. "They got a nasty sting."

The girl raised her head and gave him a look of cool disdain. The scorpion skittered rapidly toward one of her legs; at the last second she reached down, plucked it up by the tail, and tossed it into the water trough that ran the length of the porch.

While Raisy tied their horses to the hitching rail, Dryden crouched down and asked the girl if her daddy was home.

"'Course he is," she grumbled.

"We're friends of his."

"So?"

"What's your name?"

"Kit Groom," she said in an imperious voice that betokened bowing and supplication.

"Can you go and find your daddy, Kit? He's expecting us."

"What's wrong with *your* legs?" she snapped. Then, before Dryden could say anything else, she yelled, "Oh, go to the devil!" and jumped up and went running around the side of the house.

Dryden stared after her, completely flummoxed. Raisy looked amused. "Makes you want to have a couple of your own, eh?"

They looked up as the front door opened with a wheeze and a bang, and a scrawny, grizzled man came onto the porch. He was wearing faded denim overalls, dusty work boots, and nothing else.

Dryden hadn't seen Chester Groom in over twenty years, but he hadn't changed much in that time. He had the same lean, ropy body that always reminded him of beef jerky; the same sun-faded blue eyes surrounded by nests of crow's-feet; and the same tanned face that collapsed inward like a clenched fist when he smiled, like he was doing now.

"Samuel Dryden, in the flesh. God cuss it." Chester came down the porch steps and took one of Dryden's hands in his own, working it up and down like a pump-handle. "You growed up, and damned if you don't look just like your daddy."

"Chester." Dryden nodded and turned to his left. "This is my friend, Raisy."

Chester went over and shook her hand, too "Any friend of Sam's," he said, beaming. "You meet the girls?"

"We met Kit," Dryden said. "She the youngest?"

Chester snorted. "Oh yes, and the orneriest." He gave his head a wry shake. "Trying to get that girl to do her chores is like trying to herd rattlesnakes. She gets that from her mamma, I guess."

The two girls who had been tending the corn came over and stood a discrete distance away. Chester motioned at them impatiently.

"Well, come on, then. They ain't gonna bite ya."

The girls approached together. They looked to be around the same age — fourteen or fifteen, Dryden guessed. They curtsied in unison.

Chester said, "The one on the left is Hattie. The one on the right is Eudora." He raised an eyebrow at the girls. "I get it right this time?"

"Yes, sir." Their voices were as perfectly in sync as their curtsies.

"Like peas in a pod those two. You'd think they was twins, but they ain't. There's a year between 'em. Hattie's fourteen and Eudora's thirteen."

"It's nice to meet you both," Dryden said. Raisy smiled and tipped her hat. The girls stared at her in frank fascination. They looked like they were about to say something to her when Kit Groom came tearing back around the side of the house.

Chester snapped his fingers at her. "Get over here, you little demon."

Kit put on the brakes and came over to stand obediently at his side. She pointed at the saddlebag strapped to Raisy's percheron and said, "Your bag's growling."

"He doesn't like to travel," Raisy told her, "unless it's by coach." She untied the rawhide strings of the saddlebag and pulled out a lean gray tabby with bright yellow eyes.

"Da, she's got a cat!" Kit chirruped.

"She certainly does," Chester said, grinning in spite of himself. "And it don't look like a happy one, at that."

"He'll be fine," Raisy said, stroking the cat's back. It accepted this attention with cool, grudging approval.

"What's its name?" Kit asked excitedly.

"August Finch."

"What kind of name is that for a cat?"

"Yes, Raisy," Dryden said in a tone of exaggerated speculation, "what kind of name is that for a cat? Do tell."

Raisy ignored him. "It's his true name," she said to Kit. "The one a certain kind of animal keeps to itself. We found August Finch in Chicago. Or rather, he found us. At the time, we just called him 'cat.' Or as Dryden called him" — she shot him a quick glance — "that good-for-nothing cat."

Kit snickered.

"While we were passing through Chagrin Falls, Ohio, we met a carnie fortune teller who told us his true name was August Finch, and that's what we've called him ever since."

"Is that the truth?" Kit asked. She spoke in the careful, skeptical tone of a child who has heard — and believed — one tall tale too many.

"The God's honest," Raisy said. She lowered the cat so Kit could pat him, then she went up the porch steps, and tossed him into the house.

"You okay with him running around in there?" Dryden asked Chester. "You say the word and I'll put him in the corral."

"No worries," Chester said.

Raisy turned to address the Groom girls. "Dryden gets jealous because when August Finch is around he doesn't get any attention."

The girls giggled.

"Why in the world do you travel with a cat, anyway?" Chester asked.

"I ask myself that question every day," Dryden said.

Chester looked down at Kit. "Your sister could use some help with the dishes."

Kit yelled, "Devil!" and ran up the porch steps and into the house.

Ian Rogers

"Looks like you've got your hands full," Dryden observed.

Chester shook his head solemnly. "Sam, I'd need to grow three more just to deal with that little firecracker."

4

THEY met the last of the Groom girls inside the house. She was washing dishes in the kitchen. Her name was Bonnie, and at eighteen she was the oldest. Dryden and Raisy smiled and said quick hellos before Chester ushered them into the dining room and sat them at a long, scarred table under a finely-carved wooden chandelier.

"You must've been riding a long time," he said. "I'm sorry to make you come all this way. I wouldn't have sent word if things hadn't gotten so... well, desperate." He smiled uncomfortably and changed the subject. "So, I hear you're over in Utah now."

"That's right," Dryden said. "Provo."

"God bless the telegraph," Chester muttered.

Kit came in with a pitcher of iced tea and three cloudy glasses on a silver tray. She set it on the table awkwardly, almost tipping the whole works into Raisy's lap. She started to reach for the pitcher to pour the tea, but Raisy got there first. "Let me do that, honey," she said sweetly. The girl eyed her suspiciously, cast a look at Dryden, then stomped back into the kitchen.

Once she was gone, Chester sighed and said, "I don't want to dump my troubles on you right away."

Ian Rogers

Dryden leaned forward and gave Chester's shoulder a reassuring squeeze. "It's why we're here, Chester. And we're happy to help."

Chester slumped down in his seat. "This is a cattle ranch, which I guess you could tell from all the walking beef out in the corral."

They nodded.

"That in itself is part of the problem. They shouldn't be in the corral. They should be out in the pasture. I moved them in the day before yest'day. They been penned this whole time and they don't like it. Hell, *I* don't like it. Makes 'em ornery. I been making the girls stay close to the house instead of letting 'em go off and play wherever they like. And at night..." He trailed off, shaking his head. "The cattle are bawling, keeping us all awake. My knee's been acting up something fierce. Bonnie's headaches have come back. Kit's been a handful, as usual. The whole damn ranch is falling apart. Hattie and Eudora are practically running the place on their own, but they can't keep it up for long — none of us can." Chester's throat hitched and his face scrunched up to hold back the tears that wanted to come out.

Dryden nodded sympathetically. He couldn't imagine the amount of blood and sweat Chester must have put in to make a life for his family out here in the wastes of Nevada. The physical labor of maintaining a cattle ranch was hard enough, but then you threw in trying to raise four kids — four girls, no less — and it was enough to make even the strongest man buckle under the strain.

"We're going to set things right," Dryden told him. "And we'll make the ones who are killing your cattle pay." His voice went cold. "In one form or another."

Chester nodded and rubbed at his eyes. "I 'preciate that, Sam. I truly do. You coming out all this way is nothing less than a gift from God. I mean that."

"Tell me what's been happening."

Chester took a deep breath and let it out. "Okay."

"You said some of your cattle have been killed."

Chester scoffed. "That's what I put in the message I sent you. That was the only way I could describe it. But what happened to them is about as close to killin' as day is to night. Those steers was ripped to pieces."

"They were mutilated?" Raisy asked.

"That's a good word," Chester said. "It fits."

"Then maybe it isn't rustlers," she suggested. "There's no profit in killing another man's cattle. Not 'less it's a plot to take out the competition."

"Ain't no competition around here, young lady. Not another ranch for a hundred miles, and hardly any people. You been through town, ain'tcha? Little pisshole. If there's more'n fifty people in Ashes, I'll eat my boot and shit leather. That's part of the reason I set up out here in the first place."

"How many cattle have been killed?" Dryden asked.

"Three," Chester replied. "Three steers."

"Have there been any attacks since you penned them?"

Chester shook his head.

"Maybe they were killed by an animal," Raisy said.

Chester looked at her with a grave expression. "The way these cattle looked when I found 'em…" He closed his eyes and shuddered. "I don't ever want to come across the animal that done it. It ain't no coyote, that's for damn sure. I never seen any animal left in such a state. And you know what's strange? None of the carrion birds will go near 'em. These steers was dead — mutilated, as the young lady said — but the carcasses are left untouched. Like the vultures and the rest didn't want to have nothing to do with them."

"Poison?" Raisy said.

Ian Rogers

Chester shrugged his bony shoulders. "It could be that. Could be a lot of things, I guess. I can't get anyone to come out and take a proper look. That old fart who calls himself a marshal spends most of his time yakking it up with the blowhards in the barbershop."

"What's his deal?" Raisy asked. "Town's kind of small for a marshal outpost, ain't it?"

"He ain't here for the town," Chester said. "Jacobs came to Ashes just a couple of weeks ago. Don't rightly know why he's here. Says he's passing through, but if he is then he's taking his sweet ass time. Old codger's got a way of talking to you like you're about four years old."

Dryden and Raisy nodded.

"With all the hell I'm going through these days, I don't much care why he's here. He come out to look at them dead steers and he told me it was probably predators." Chester shook his head. "Man's as useless as a pecker on a pope."

"Don't worry about it," Dryden said. "We're going to check it out."

Chester nodded. "I got a place you can start. I burned the first two steer I found, but I left the last one. It's still out there right where I found it. I figured no point in moving it. It ain't going nowhere."

"We'll head out and take a look," Dryden said.

"Might want to grab a bite before you go," Chester said. "You ain't liable to have much of an appetite afterwards."

5

ALL four of the Groom girls came out to see off Dryden and Raisy

"Just head out due west into the pasture," Chester said. "It's a couple hours' ride, but you won't have any trouble finding it." He stuck a rusted metal canister into one of Dryden's saddlebags. "You'll need that for later."

Dryden and Raisy touched spurs and headed out at a lope. They were both amazed at how quickly the land turned from the flat interminable stretch of the dry lakebed to the patchy brush of the pasture.

They were getting hot and tired as they day dragged on.

"I don't understand why he didn't just come out here and show us," Raisy said gruffly.

"He doesn't want to leave his kids alone," Dryden said. "He's circled the wagons and now he's holding tight until the trouble either goes away or comes down on top of him with both feet. He—"

"Wait."

Raisy was staring at a wide expanse of chaparral a short distance away. Something was sticking out of it at an odd angle. At first glance it looked like a scrub tree, but as she clucked her horse closer, she saw it was an animal's leg sticking up in the air.

She drew up and looked down with mingled curiosity and disgust. The leg was attached to a section of thigh which itself was attached to nothing at all. Dryden came up next to her.

"Good Lord," he muttered, and crossed himself.

Chester was right. Saying that the steer had been killed was like saying the Grand Canyon was only a hole in the ground. Something much worse had happened here. Something that could not be adequately described by words like "killed" or even "mutilated." To Dryden it looked like someone had lit a stick of dynamite and shoved it down the steer's throat.

The remains were barely recognizable as something that had once been a living, breathing animal. The only part that bore any resemblance to a steer was the head, which they found lying on its side in a pool of dry blood. One glassy, red-filmed eye stared out sightlessly.

Raisy reached into her coat and came out with a long hunting knife. She used it to turn the head over. "Yep," she said, "it's dead."

"You're a laff riot, Raisy."

"I don't think a person did this. Not unless this is how they get their kicks. I don't see the point."

"An animal attack, then?"

Raisy turned her head and stared at a line of low hills on the horizon. "Maybe. Or maybe that's just how someone wanted it to look."

"How's that?"

Raisy stood up, wiped her knife on her sleeve, and put it back in her coat. "This is a nasty piece of work," she said. "It could have been an animal done it, but it doesn't quite fit." She tapped a piece of tattered flesh with her boot. "I see plenty of meat lying around and no teeth marks on any of it."

Dryden nodded grimly. "Chester was right about the carrion birds. This place should be a goddamn vulture convention, but there ain't a one."

With looks of barely-restrained nausea on their faces, Dryden and Raisy kicked and prodded the pieces of the steer into a pile. Dryden fetched the canister Chester had given them and unscrewed the cap. The pungent smell of gasoline filled the air. Dryden upended the canister and doused the pile. Raisy scratched a wooden match on the bottom of her boot and dropped it on the remains.

They stood in silence as the steer went up in flames. The heat blanketed them, but they still felt a chill, as if there was a part of themselves that could never be warmed.

Ian Rogers

6

AFTER dinner that evening, while the Groom girls were cleaning up, Dryden and Raisy sat down with Chester to discuss what they had seen that day and what they should do next.

"The other dead steers," Dryden began without preamble, "were they in the same condition as the one we saw today?"

Chester nodded. "My daddy once told me that if you're gonna have livestock, then you're gonna have deadstock. But I never expected anything like this. It's like something out of a nightmare."

"What do you think we should do?" Dryden asked him.

Chester looked at him strangely for a moment, then he said, "You don't have any ideas?" He sounded almost crestfallen.

"I have a few," Dryden said, "and we'll run with them on our own, but I don't want to leave you sitting here waiting to see what's going to happen next. This is your ranch, Chester, and I'm not going to presume to know what's in your own best interests. I want to know what *you* think should be done here."

Chester settled back in his seat and thought about it for a good long time. Finally he said, "Well, I can't keep the cattle

Ian Rogers

locked up forever. I guess the first thing I'd like to do is let them out. Maybe you and Raisy can go out with them. Camp tender out in the pasture and keep an eye on 'em through the night. See if there's someone or something out there that's been waiting for them to come back."

Dryden nodded. "That's about what I figured, too."

Chester got his oldest girl, Bonnie, to help him open the corral gate and move the cattle out into the yard. They came slowly, almost warily. They were used to moving out at the start of the day rather than at the end of it. They mooed loudly and nudged one another along like a throng of cranky children.

After Chester and Bonnie had herded them around to the back of the house, Dryden and Raisy took over. With their bedrolls tied to their saddles, they rode up on either side of the cattle and led them out to the pasture. In the distance, the sun was going down in a blaze of pastel reds and oranges.

By the time they set up camp, not far from the place where they had burned the dead steer, the sky had turned an eerie violet color. They decided not to build another fire. If there was someone or something out there, they didn't want to announce their presence.

Dryden took the first watch. He paced around their small camp to keep from falling asleep. He was exhausted from the ride to Nevada, and he knew that a man could fall asleep standing on his feet if he was tired enough. He stared out into the darkening night. The cattle grazed and snorted and whipped their tails. Dryden went out and walked among them, trying to distinguish any movement or sound that didn't belong. He didn't notice anything unusual.

Two hours later, Dryden crawled into his bedroll and Raisy took her turn on watch. She took out a knife with a weighted haft and twirled it in her hand. She looked around for something to throw it at, but there were no trees around, only a few struggling scrub bushes and some cholla. She sighed and kept twirling the knife back and forth between her fingers.

The night went by without incident. Dryden was back on watch when the sun came creeping up in the east. He woke up Raisy by nudging her with his boot. She grumbled under her breath and rolled onto her back.

"Get up, sunshine."

"I wanna sleep in a bed," she mumbled grumpily.

"You'll get one tonight. Whoever or whatever killed those cattle doesn't seem to want to come out while we're here. Looks like we'll have to try another approach."

Raisy stood up and stretched the kinks out of her arms and legs. "You want to pick another spot — on the high ground maybe?"

Dryden shook his head. "If it's an animal doing this, then it's a smart one. Probably got our scent and decided to lay low. It'll smell us out as long as we stick close to the cattle. No sense staying away if—" He broke off.

"What is it?" Raisy followed his gaze out into the herd. "You see something?"

Instead of replying, Dryden strode briskly forward into the herd. His coat was open and his hand rested on the greenwood grip of his revolver. Raisy drew a pair of knives and followed after him. She started to say something and Dryden hissed at her.

They zigzagged through the cattle that stood around like a wandering maze. Dryden came around a one-horned steer and stopped in his tracks.

"Shit."

Raisy came up next to him and felt all her breath come out in a startled gasp.

The mutilated carcass of a steer was spread across a small circular clearing about twenty feet in diameter. None of the other cattle crossed into this space, as if it were protected by some invisible barrier.

"How..." Raisy began.

Dryden scanned the horizon in every direction, but he didn't see anything. No trails cut through the foliage; there was no dust cloud kicked up by horses; nothing.

"How could this happen?" Raisy said angrily. "We been here all night." She crouched next to the edge of the killing circle and dipped her fingertips in a puddle of blood. It was still warm. "This just happened." She ran her fingers through the dusty ground to clean them. She caught Dryden's look and gestured at the gun on his hip. "You didn't get anything?"

Dryden shook his head. He looked down at the dead steer's entrails spread across the ground in long, grisly lengths. They were steaming in the cool, early-morning air.

"The steer didn't make a sound," he stated firmly. "We would've heard it. It's only fifty feet from where we set up camp."

"You think they knew we were out here?"

Dryden nodded.

"They didn't seem too concerned about us," Raisy said.

Dryden's eyes narrowed. "That's the part that scares me."

7

AFTER burning the dead steer, Dryden and Raisy left the herd to graze and headed back to the ranch. If whatever was killing the cattle wanted to take another one, it would probably do so whether or not they were around to keep watch.

They had surveyed the area around the dead steer, but hadn't found any footprints or animal tracks or any other disturbances that would suggest that something had infiltrated the herd. Raisy did find something in the sand — a small, dusty brush, like the kind a prospector might use to brush away dirt — but neither she nor Dryden thought it was the murder weapon. They were, in short, baffled.

They didn't speak on the ride back. Instead they consulted with their own thoughts, trying to make some sense of the previous night and comb their minds for any clue that they might have disregarded.

As they came up to the ranch, Raisy spotted a small dark shape beyond the house, off toward the dry lakebed on the far side of the property. After a moment, Dryden saw it too. They exchanged a wordless glance and spurred their horses forward.

The shape became a person. The person became a woman. A naked woman.

"Good morning," Dryden muttered to himself as they slowed down and took in the tall, curvaceous form of Bonnie Groom. She was walking back and forth across the dry, cracked ground, naked as a newborn babe, looking around as if she had lost something.

Raisy shook her head pityingly. "That poor man," she said. "This whole thing keeps getting stranger and stranger."

Dryden nodded grimly. Chester wasn't kidding when he said the ranch was falling down around him. He had raised free-range daughters, but for the last few weeks he had been keeping them penned, and now they were finally showing the strain of it. Here was a young woman who had grown so claustrophobic that she even found her clothes too confining.

"Bonnie?"

She turned and looked at them with wide, startled eyes. "I'm looking for treasure," she said in a querulous voice. "There's silver around here."

Raisy rode forward a bit. "Have you seen any prospectors around here?"

Bonnie went back to scanning the ground. "I seen riders go by the house one night a while back. They was heading for the Cemetery Hills. Jesse and me used to play out there," she added in a low, secretive voice.

"When did you see them, honey?"

She seemed to consider this for a moment, then shook her head. "Can't remember. Last week. Last month. I don't know."

"Who's Jesse?" Dryden asked.

She lowered her eyes. "My sister," she said. "She died when she was sixteen. She went out to fetch water from the pump one morning, and there was a rattlesnake in the bucket. I told her not to go, but she said Pa would give her a whuppin' if she didn't. So she went and she never got another whuppin'. Not ever again." She covered her mouth with both hands and started sobbing.

"Bonnie, let's go home, okay?"

Dryden unfastened his bedroll and passed it to Raisy, who dismounted and went over to the girl. She put the blankets around the girl's shoulders and led her back to the horse. Raisy helped her up into the saddle and they headed to the ranch.

Chester and the rest of his girls were standing on the porch when they came into the yard. Kit came down the steps and started bugling, "Bonnie's in the altogether! Bonnie's in the altogether!"

"Quiet," Chester said in a low, firm voice, and Kit immediately stopped. She ran around the side of the house laughing, while Eudora and Hattie came over to help Bonnie off the horse.

"Take her up to her room," Chester told them, and the three girls went silently into the house.

"We found her wandering out on the lakebed," Dryden explained as he and Raisy tied up their horses.

"She's an odd stick, that one," Chester said. "Always been a bit loopy. I'd like to blame it on the sun or on account of she don't have no friends her own age, but it's just the way she is. Every man has his cross, I suppose, and I have my Bonnie."

"You're gonna want to keep an eye on her," Dryden said. "This isn't a good time to be wandering around alone."

Chester nodded. "I don't mean to apologize for her. She's not crazy. I seen crazy. Years back, after we first settled here, we used to keep chickens. Not many, just a couple dozen broilers, enough to keep us in eggs and the occasional chicken dinner. We had a dog to watch over 'em. Didn't have a name; we just called him The Dog." He sat down on the porch step and his knees popped like pineknots in a fireplace. "One day he up and vanished. I figured he'd taken off as some dogs are apt to do. Then, a few days later, a couple of the chickens turned up dead. The next day I found a few more, blood and feathers all across the yard near the coup. It weren't nearly as bad as how those cattle looked, but it was pretty bad. Hattie had nightmares for weeks." He shook his head at the unpleasant memory. "One night I stayed out on the porch with my rifle and waited. Eventually the dog came trotting out of the night, as I knew it would. It wasn't walking so good, and I could see the foam around its mouth."

"Hydrophobia," Dryden said in a low voice, and Chester nodded.

"Yeah, no coming back from that. I shot the dog without hesitation. But the look in his eyes when he saw me sitting there waiting for him." Chester ran a hand across his craggy face. "I was between him and those chickens, and he was ready to tear my throat out to get at 'em. There was no hesitation in those eyes. So I put him down. Because that's what a man has to do sometimes to protect his family, his home. I don't know what it is that's killing those cattle, but I can tell you this: Whatever it is, it's as crazy as that dog. Only difference is, unlike that dog, I can't do nothing about it."

"You can do something for your girls," Raisy told him. "Let us worry about the other."

After hearing Chester's story about the rabid dog and his inability to handle his current situation, Dryden was reluctant to tell him about what had happened last night. But he did. He explained why they'd left the cattle in the pasture, and Chester nodded wanly. Dryden said he and Raisy could bring them back to the corral, but Chester waved a dismissive hand.

"If you bring 'em back in then we're right back where we started. Leaving the herd out there might provoke whatever's killing 'em."

"You want to use your cattle as bait?" Raisy said, unable to keep the incredulous note out of her voice.

"I want to get to the bottom of this, young lady," Chester said, a bit tersely. "And this seems to be the only way to do that."

Raisy looked over at Dryden. Dryden gave her a barely perceptible nod, then turned to Chester.

"Your daughter mentioned seeing some men riding out toward a place called the Cemetery Hills. Are those the same hills I saw out beyond the pasture?"

"That's right," Chester said. "The girls used to play over there when I was out with the herd. There's a few caves, nothing too special about them, though."

"You ever heard of prospectors in this area?" Raisy asked.

Chester shook his head. "No. Not much out here worth anything."

"Not even in those caves?"

"I check 'em out once, just to make sure it was safe for the girls to play in 'em, but there's not much to them. Only three or four caves in total, and none go deeper into the hills than maybe a quarter mile. Hardly worth the effort for a prospecting crew to come out all this way."

Dryden nodded in agreement. "We're heading out again tonight."

Raisy leaned toward him and whispered, "I thought I was going to sleep in a bed tonight."

"You can stay if you want," Dryden said, "but I wanna take a look at those caves."

Raisy sighed and looked off into the west.

Ian Rogers

8

THERE were no more mutilated cattle when they rejoined the herd. Dryden thanked God for small favors. As night fell, they decided to build a fire since there wasn't much point in trying to keep a low profile anymore. Whatever was killing the cattle it clearly knew they were in the area and didn't seem to perceive them to be much of a threat.

Raisy didn't raise much of a fuss about the lack of a bed as long as she was warm. She had stopped grumbling by the time Dryden laid down for the first rest break of the night. He watched her pacing around the fire, her shadow stretching out long and dark like an extension of her frock coat.

He woke up an unknown time later by something pulling at his waist. At first he thought it was Raisy waking him up for his turn on watch, but when he finally, grudgingly, opened his eyes, he didn't see anyone there. He looked down at his waist and his breath caught in his throat.

His gun was straining against the confines of its holster as if it were being tugged by an invisible rope. His hips gave an involuntary thrust with each effort.

Ian Rogers

"Samuel Dryden, ain't you a sight," Raisy said, and laughed from where she was standing near the cherry-red embers of their smoldering campfire.

Dryden rose clumsily to his feet, holding his hands out and away from his gunbelt. "I don't care how many times I see it happen..." He trailed off as he allowed himself to be led out into the night. Raisy shook her head in amusement and followed him, pulling the horses along by their bridle reins.

The gun led them north away from the slumbering herd. Raisy kept turning back and looking for the glow of their fire, using it as a focal point to determine exactly where they were headed — and more importantly, how to get back.

Up ahead, Dryden said, "Whoa, whoa," as if he were reining in a truculent mare. Raisy looked past him and felt her breath catch in her throat.

They had reached the Cemetery Hills. They had materialized out of the night like giant fangs that longed to devour the stars. At the foot of the hills were the entrances to three caves, standing out like the eye sockets of some enormously misshapen three-eyed skull.

Dryden finally reached down and pulled the gun out of its holster. It jerked in his hand and almost flew out of his grip.

Raisy said, "I think it wants us to go inside."

Dryden shot her a sarcastic look. "You think so?"

Raisy stared at the three caves and tapped a finger thoughtfully against her lips. "But which one?"

Dryden planted his feet more firmly on the ground. Then, as if sensing his resistance, the gun gave a powerful lurch and his arm snapped out in the direction of the middle cave.

"Ask and ye shall receive."

Raisy raised her hands in an after-you gesture.

Dryden started forward. Raisy ground-hitched their horses and followed him. At the cave entrance, she stopped, crouched down, and stirred the sand with one black-gloved finger. "Tracks here," she muttered. "Three people. No horses."

Dryden's eyebrows drew together in puzzlement. "They walked out here?"

Raisy shrugged. "We did."

They entered the cave. A few feet in, Dryden glimpsed the dark shape of something hanging on a metal hook that had been pounded into the stone wall. He motioned to Raisy and she went over to take a look. It was an old lantern. She lifted it off the hook by its rusty handle and squinted into the smoke-stained glass bowl. "I think there's still oil in it," she said.

"Then light it up so we can see where the hell we're going."

She took out a wooden match and lit the lantern, using the adjustment knob to increase the glow of the flame. Even at its strongest setting it cast only a dim glow.

The gun gave another momentous tug in Dryden's hand, propelling him forward. Raisy came up quickly alongside him with the lantern held in one outstretched hand. She tried to move ahead of him so she could light their way, but ended up stumbling over something on the ground. She threw out her free hand and clutched at the cave wall to keep from falling. When she had regained her balanced, she crouched down to see what had tripped her up.

The greasy glow of the lantern illuminated the supine body of a young man. He was dead, Raisy saw. His clothes were covered in blood, but it didn't appear to be his own. But he was definitely dead. His eyes had been ripped out.

"Dryden..." She moved the lantern slowly along the length of the body. When she didn't get an answer, she turned around and looked for him. They had entered a chamber of indeterminable size; the glow of the lantern wasn't strong enough to reveal how big it was. Dryden was an indistinct shape about fifteen paces away. He was staring at the gun in his hand as if seeing it for the first time. Then he turned his head and looked at Raisy with a quizzical expression on his face.

"It stopped."

"Get over here, Dryden."

Dryden came over and stared down at the body. "Looks like whoever or whatever we're dealing with isn't restricting themselves to cattle," he commented.

"Nice to know they don't discriminate." Raisy wrinkled her nose as the lantern illuminated his face. "Just a young fella, from the look of him. He doesn't look like the steer we saw yesterday, but there's got to be a connection."

The dead man abruptly sat up, almost knocking the lantern out of Raisy's hand. "Christ!" she swore and stumbled backward. The dead man turned his head in her direction, seeming to have no trouble finding her even though he didn't have any eyes in his head. Faster than she could react, he reached out and grabbed her ankle. Raisy tried to pull away, but the thing's grip was as cold and strong as a metal clamp. He drew her toward him with a mighty yank. Dryden caught her and tried to pull her free, but the dead man swatted him away with a casual backhand that sent him flying across the chamber.

Raisy dropped the lantern and rolled onto her side, bringing up her other foot and kicking the dead man square in the face. He still didn't let go.

Dryden climbed unsteadily to his feet. He touched the back of his head and winced. He started back at a stumbling trot and glimpsed something off to his left. He looked in that direction as a shadow rose up before him. A man-shaped shadow.

It came at Dryden. He tried to level his pistol, but his attacker grabbed him and swung him around in a crazy dance. Up close he saw this man was about as young as the one Raisy had stumbled over, and just as dead. This one still had his eyes, but his throat was a ragged mess of torn flesh that hung down like a tattered bandanna.

Raisy gave her eyeless attacker another kick, this one in the chest, and sent him tumbling ass over teapot into the corner. She spun away, dipping one hand into her coat and coming out with a long stiletto. She flung it across the chamber at the dead man wresting with Dryden. It stuck in his back, but didn't seem to have any effect.

Raisy leaped to her feet and came striding across the chamber. She pulled the knife out of the dead man's back, looked at it briefly, then slipped it back into her coat. His clothes were similar to those of his eyeless friend. They were drenched in blood; more blood than his wounds warranted. It looked like they had found their cattle mutilators.

"You gonna help me or what?" Dryden asked, grimacing.

"I'm working on it," Raisy said. She drew a long bowie knife — the biggest one she carried — and then the darkness on her right side shifted and another dead man came at her.

He moved quickly — a tall, rawboned man who might have been handsome before all the skin on his face had been scraped off. Like the other two men, his blood-drenched clothes gave him the appearance of someone who worked in an abattoir. Raisy swung her bowie knife in an upward motion, slicing him open from groin to neck, and then down and across in a broad stroke that opened his stomach. The dead man's intestines flopped out like a mass of rotten sausage links. He didn't seem to notice as he reached out toward Raisy with his gore-stained fingers.

"Goddamn ghouls," she hissed.

The one attacking Dryden had pulled him into a tight embrace. Its jaws snapped open and closed like the pistons of a machine. Dryden used his free hand to keep the ghoul from tearing his throat out. The other hand was still holding the revolver. The greenwood grip was getting hot. Very hot. He tightened his hold on it and felt his flesh begin to scald and burn. With a primal growl he jammed the muzzle under the ghoul's chin. He curled his finger around the trigger and felt a draining sensation run through his entire body. As he pulled the trigger back, the feeling became a searing, crushing pain like his heart was being squeezed between a pair of burning hands.

The chamber was empty, but the gun still fired.

There was a portentous boom, like thunder, and the ghoul was propelled upward on a curling tongue of green fire that lit up the entire chamber. The ghoul's skull struck the rocky ceiling and exploded. Dryden covered his head as a shower of brain tissue and bone shards rained down on him.

He looked over at Raisy as she swung her own attacker around in a half-circle and flipped him over her shoulder. He holstered his gun — noticing absently that the 14 burned into the grip had changed to 13 — and went over to her.

"You okay?"

"Oh, sure," Raisy said, breathing heavily. "I'm as right as a trivet."

The two remaining ghouls — Eyeless and Faceless — shambled toward them.

"Don't let them bite you," Dryden said, "unless you want to start keeping different company."

"You got any ideas?"

"Try silver."

"They're not were-critters."

"Just try it."

Raisy let out a frustrated breath and withdrew a knife with slender, four-inch blade. It gleamed milkily in the low, throbbing glow of the lantern. She looked quickly between the two ghouls advancing on them, then threw the knife at the eyeless one. The knife struck in the center of its peeling forehead. The ghoul kept coming on, totally unfazed.

Raisy looked down at the pistol in Dryden's hand. "Can you use that again?"

Dryden considered it, then shook his head. "Not tonight. I'd probably pass out."

"Then we're at a stalemate."

"For now."

They backtracked quickly out of the cave. They took turns covering their retreat, but the two ghouls didn't seem to be following them. Outside, they swung up into their saddles and high-tailed it away from the Cemetery Hills.

"You think they'll come for us?" Raisy asked.

Dryden looked at the hot pink line on the eastern horizon that signaled the coming sunrise.

"Not during the day," he said. "But tonight? I'd bet money on it."

Once they were back at their camp, they packed up quickly. While Dryden was kicking sand over the coals of their fire, he said, "Do you think they were the riders Bonnie was talking about?"

Raisy shrugged. "I forgot to ask them."

"I guess it doesn't matter. It doesn't explain how they got to being the way they are, or why they killed those cattle."

"They owe me a knife." Raisy opened her coat and stared inside longingly. "I'm down to fifty-one now."

The moment the words left her mouth she was overcome by a sudden feeling of prescience. Something about that number and this place.

"At least we know why we never found any tracks," Dryden said as he climbed back onto his mount.

Raisy shook her head, clearing her thoughts. "We do?"

"The whole time they were attacking us, their feet never touched the ground." Dryden looked at her wonderingly. "Didn't you notice?"

"To be honest," Raisy said, "I wasn't really looking."

9

THE following day, Chester brought the cattle back into the corral. Dryden and Raisy told him they were going back out to camp in the pasture. Chester didn't ask them why — he had grown progressively more sullen and detached over the past three days — and Dryden and Raisy didn't say. They took August Finch with them this time. Dryden was against it, but Raisy insisted. She didn't like the idea of leaving him alone with Kit Groom. Earlier that day, Raisy had caught the girl trying to tie a bonnet on the cat's head.

"Who ever heard of riding with a cat?" Dryden asked that evening as they rode out to the pasture.

"I don't know why he gets on your nerves so much," Raisy said.

"He snores!"

"He does not!" Raisy said indignantly. "No louder than you."

"I ask you, who ever heard of riding with a cat?"

"You used to say the same thing about women."

Dryden grumbled under his breath.

Ian Rogers

They set up camp a good distance away from both the ranch and the Cemetery Hills. Dryden built a fire while Raisy went off on her errand. She came back an hour later with a dead rabbit. She sat down next to Dryden and proceeded to gut and skin it.

"I don't understand why we need to go through this every time," she said.

"It's procedure," Dryden said vaguely.

Raisy sighed. "Can you hurry up and call the wolf? I'd like to get this over with."

"You know it has to be done. We need to get the dope on these ghouls so we don't get euchred again."

"I'm not disagreeing with you, Dryden, I just don't like it."

Dryden let his eyes drift to the fire. He fixed his gaze on the flickering flames and began to concentrate. His eyelids drooped to half-mast. He got lost in the changing colors. Red, orange, yellow. Orange, yellow, red. Yellow, red, orange. He felt a light tugging sensation not unlike the way the greenwood gun had pulled at him. Except this one was tugging at his mind. He felt something detach from him. It was completely painless, and yet he felt a sense of loss and loneliness. He was drifting through the air over the desert floor. He could feel the stars above him like burning pinpricks on his back. The moon was a silver spotlight. He looked down at the ground and saw another moon. No, not the moon. It was too shiny. He came in closer and saw Bonnie Groom, naked and digging again. She was pulling up chunks of the dry lakebed with her bare hands. She had uncovered something, a large section of some enormous metallic object. "What is that?" he called down to her. She looked up at him and yelled, "It's the dish! The supper dish! Can't you hear them calling us to supper?" He cocked his head to the side and heard a low rumbling that quickly rose to a thunderous rending sound. The ground began to tremble and the cracked pieces of the lakebed began to leap into the air, exposing more and more of the burnished metal underneath. "They're calling!" Bonnie screamed. Her voice flowed seamlessly into a loud, wavering howl that split the night in two.

Dryden's eyes sprang open. He stared out across the fire, past Raisy who sat with her eyes squinched shut and her hands covering her ears, to a glowing shape that trotted slowly, almost casually, out of the darkness. The shape resolved itself into the form of a wolf with yellow orbs for eyes and fur that glowed with a silver radiance.

Raisy opened her eyes and lowered her hands. She watched as the wolf came up alongside her and nudged the dead rabbit with its snout.

"Good," it said in a deep, gravelly voice. It looked up at her and seemed to grin. "Very good."

Raisy kept silent as it picked the rabbit up in its jaws and carried it over to a spot on the other side of the fire. It dropped the skinned and gutted carcass on the ground and sat down.

Dryden rasped, "Marmen..."

The wolf raised its head and looked at him. "What did you see, Samuel Dryden?"

Dryden told the wolf about his vision — flying over the desert at night, Bonnie Groom naked and digging, the silver object under the lakebed.

"She called it a dish."

"Did she?" The wolf's ears perked up. "It's of no consequence. She doesn't know what it really is. She has the long sight, but can't see what's right in front of her. And she's crazy. That muddies the waters."

"Did the long sight make her crazy?"

"I don't know," Marmen said ruminatively. "I can't see. But never mind her, and never mind the dish. That's a problem for another time. There are more immediate concerns to deal with."

Raisy said, "The ghouls," and the wolf nodded.

"They have been brought back against the natural laws. They will not rest until order has been restored."

"How can we do that?" Dryden asked.

"With fire," Marmen said in a throaty growl. "You must destroy them utterly and completely. They will remain on earth for as long as they posses earthly remains."

August Finch crawled out of Raisy's bedroll. He took one look at Marmen and hissed at him.

"Oh, shut your big bazoo," the wolf said, and August Finch slunk back under the blankets.

"So we need to burn the ghouls?" Raisy said.

"Burn them," Marmen said, "and scatter the ashes in the wind."

The wolf cocked its head to one side, as if listening to some distant sound. "These undead are wary of you, Samuel Dryden. They fear the greenwood gun, as all unnaturals do. They will not attack this night. But they cannot deny the calling."

"What calling?" Raisy asked.

Marmen ignored her. "They will strike tomorrow after the sun dies in the west. Be ready!"

Dryden nodded.

The wolf lowered its head and sniffed the dead rabbit.

"One last thing."

"Yes?"

"Do you have any potatoes?"

10

ON the ride back to the ranch, with the rising sun dragging their shadows out long behind them, Dryden and Raisy tried to figure out what had caused all of these events to transpire. The mutilations, the madness, the monsters. There must have been some catalyst that set the whole thing into motion.

"Maybe it's the caves," Raisy suggested. "It could be a dark place. You remember Seven Stones Valley?"

Dryden nodded. He felt a pang of horror as he closed his eyes and pictured Willy Raglan coming out of the spring at the center of the Seven Stones. He had looked all right at first. Then he took a couple of steps and sort of fell to pieces. His teeth poured out of his mouth in a fountain of blood and syrupy pink stuff that used to be his gums. The flesh fell off his hands as he raised them up to a face from which all the skin suddenly slid off. His eyes, staring beseechingly at Dryden and Raisy, spilled out of their sockets and ran down his cheeks like grisly tears. He managed to take one more step forward and then collapsed in a pile of bones wrapped in gore-drenched clothing. One leather boot remained standing, and when Dryden tipped it over a grisly stew that used to be Willy Raglan's foot had poured out.

"Or maybe it's the lakebed," Raisy went on. "That's where we found Bonnie out digging that day."

Dryden thought about it for a long moment. "I think this entire basin is contaminated — from the lakebed to the Cemetery Hills — and I've got a feeling the dish, whatever it is, is the cause."

"Marmen said it wasn't our problem."

"I know," Dryden said, "but I think those ghouls might have been prospectors before they joined the ranks of the undead, and I think they found something in those caves. Something... wrong."

"Chester said his girls used to play out there all the time. How come nothing happened to them?"

"Does Bonnie seem right as a rail to you?"

Raisy frowned. "Maybe those men dug something up. Something like the dish. Maybe it poisoned 'em and brought 'em back to life."

"That's a lot of maybes."

"Chester should just take his girls and leave," Raisy said firmly. "They can stay in Ashes until we settle this. Then they should pull up stakes and start over somewhere else. You said it yourself, Dryden, this place is 'taminated."

Dryden was shaking his head before she had finished talking. "It's no good," he told her grimly. "Chester'll no sooner leave his land than he would leave his girls. Whatever happens tonight, they're gonna be caught right in the middle of it."

"What can we do?"

Dryden looked at her with cool, steady eyes. "We move the fight away from the ranch."

"Back to the caves?" Raisy said warily.

"No, that would give them the advantage. And we can't wait for them in the pasture because they might go around us and head straight to the ranch. They could do it, too; there's a lot of wide open space out there. I think the only course of action is to put Chester and the girls in the house, board it up, and wait for the ghouls in the yard. Make it so they have to get through us first."

"A welcoming party," Raisy said. "I like it. In a dead run, suicidal sort of way."

Dryden nodded. "We'll give 'em what for, or die trying."

They put the plan to Chester and he grudgingly agreed. Dryden was right: Chester didn't want to leave the ranch, but he didn't want to put his daughters in harm's way, either. Strangely, he didn't seem to have any trouble accepting the fact that the men responsible for killing his cattle weren't really men at all. He told Dryden that he had seen his share of "Injun ha'nts," and left it at that.

They immediately set to work on boarding up the windows and doors. They left the front door for last. Dryden and Raisy would secure it once the sun went down.

They had most of the work done by the late afternoon. The Groom girls lugged planks and tools while Dryden, Raisy, and Chester did the grunt work. Chester asked why they bothered to board up the second-story windows. Dryden considered telling him the ghouls could levitate, then simply said, "It's best to cover all our bases."

When they were done, Kit Groom went to fetch a bucket of water to cool everyone off. Dryden decided to go with her. Just before they reached the pump, he told her to hang back a bit, then stepped forward and tipped the wooden bucket over with one outstretched foot. He'd been unable to shake the image of Jesse Groom getting bit by a rattlesnake.

"They ate her eyes," Kit said brightly.

Dryden looked down at her, confused. "Who did?"

Ian Rogers

"The vultures!" Kit said as if it were obvious. "I seen them do it. Pa scared them away. Then he took Jessie on his horse into town, but she was already dead." She looked at the bucket lying on its side. "If any snake tries to bite me, I'd knock its lights out."

I'm sure you would, Dryden thought as he started working the pump-handle. *I think you'd give that snake a real run for its money.*

11

THEY had an early dinner, but no one was very hungry. Everyone picked listlessly at their food. Afterward, Chester helped the girls clear the table while Dryden and Raisy went out on the porch. They walked around to the back and stared off into the west.

"It'll be dark within the hour," Dryden said.

They went back around to the front and lit the lanterns Chester had rustled up. There were ten of them. They put one in the house and positioned the other nine around the yard. It didn't illuminate the entire property, but it was better than nothing. Chester had refilled the gas can and left it out near the gate of the corral.

While Dryden and Raisy were getting their horses ready, the front door slammed open and Bonnie Groom came flying down the porch steps and across the yard. She was tearing at her clothes like they were on fire and screaming at the top of her lungs. *"The dish! The dish!"* She ran past the corral in the direction of the dry lakebed.

Ian Rogers

Dryden and Raisy mounted up and tore off after her. She was moving fast, but they were on horseback and she wasn't, and it took only a matter of minutes to catch up to her.

"Bonnie!" Dryden yelled. "You have to go back to the house. It ain't safe out here."

Bonnie fell on her knees at the edge of the dusty, cracked ground and began pulling up pieces of the dry, brittle earth. "The dish will protect me," she said. "The dish will save me."

"We haven't got time for this," Raisy said impatiently. She slid off her mount and grabbed Bonnie roughly by the upper arms. The girl struggled in her grip and Raisy released one arm so she could slap her across the face. A semblance of sanity seemed to come back into Bonnie's eyes, and she glared at the other woman with a burning hate. She started to struggle again.

"Let me go!"

Raisy slapped again, backhanded this time, and Bonnie swooned. Dryden climbed off his horse and together they laid her across the horn of his saddle.

Raisy went back to her house grumbling. "When we get back I'm going to lash her to the goddam—"

The sound of a gunshot shattered the still air.

"Dammit," Dryden leaped into his saddle and wheeled around. "If those bastards were waiting for a distraction, I think we just gave 'em one."

Raisy swung back onto her mount and they hightailed it back to the ranch.

Two of the ghouls — the one with no face and the one Dryden had shot — were up on the porch. They were trying to tear off the boards covering one of the front windows. The third ghoul — the eyeless one with a silver knife sticking out of its forehead — was standing in the yard. Waiting for them.

"Die," Bonnie moaned. "Everybody die."

56

"We can't fight them and keep an eye on her at the same time," Dryden said. "One of us will have to keep those things busy while the other takes her into the house." He started to say that he would hold off the ghouls, but Raisy was already off her house and walking toward the one in the yard.

"Raisy," Dryden hissed, "what in the hell are you doing?"

She didn't stop walking. Her words drifted back to him.

"I'm going to get my knife back."

Dryden spurred his horse onward, giving the eyeless ghoul a wide berth, and headed toward the house. He rode fast and made it to the porch steps in a matter of seconds. The ghouls didn't seem to notice them. Dryden climbed off his horse, got Bonnie down, and dragged her up the steps. He pounded on the door and bellowed, "Chester! It's Sam! Let us in!"

The door was jerked open an agonizing second later and Dryden shoved Bonnie inside. He followed her in, and Chester slammed the door closed behind them. A moment later, they heard one of the ghouls coming down on it with both fists.

Chester clutched a double-barrel shotgun in his hands. Dryden pushed Bonnie at him and said, "Take her upstairs and stay there."

Outside, Raisy was striding purposefully across the yard when she spied a coiled lasso hanging off one of the fence posts. She went over and picked it up, testing the weight in her hands. She paid out a little slack and started twirling it. She began with small, quick circles, then, as she built up speed, worked up to wider circles as she brought it up over her head. The eyeless ghoul lurched soundlessly toward her. Dryden was right. Their feet really didn't touch the ground.

When it was about twenty feet away, she let fly and the lasso landed neatly around the ghoul's neck and left shoulder. She clinched it tight. The ghoul grabbed the rope in both hands and pulled. Raisy was snapped off her feet and landed on the ground

57

in a cloud of dust. She stood up quickly and tied the rope to one of the fence posts, anchoring the ghoul to the corral as neatly as a dog on a lead. Still holding its end of the rope, the ghoul suddenly reached up and used the blade of the knife still sticking out of its forehead to cut itself free.

Raisy stared in blank surprise. "And here I thought you were just a walking slab of meat with an attitude."

The ghoul advanced on her with its arms outstretched. She picked up the gas can and cursed herself for not leaving the cap unscrewed. She tried to work it open, but it was screwed on tight and the ghoul was coming at her fast. When it was within striking distance, she swung the can upward and caught the ghoul under the chin. She brought it around again in an awkward sideways blow that knocked the ghoul back a few steps. It was only dazed for a moment, but that was all Raisy needed. She dropped the gas can and picked up one of the lanterns hanging on a hook in a fence post. Holding it by the wire handle, she swung it in a wide, overhand blow. The glass container came down on the ghoul's head, shattering the bowl and splashing oil on both of them. The ghoul immediately went up in flames. Raisy leaped clear, but the arms of her frock coat were already burning. She slipped out of it quickly and stamped out the flames.

The ghoul flailed around madly. It took a step toward Raisy, started to take another, then crumbled to the ground in a burning pile.

Raisy slipped her coat back on while she watched it burn. Then she reached down, pulled her knife out of the flaming skull, and ran back to the house with the smoke from her coat trailing behind her.

12

DRYDEN looked back and forth between the front door and the window. There was a ghoul banging on each of them. He touched the butt of his gun and silently wished he had asked Chester for the use of his shotgun.

He went into the living room and was looking around for something he could use as a weapon when the front door split down the center and the boards over the window exploded inwardly. The ghouls clambered inside. The one that came through the door was the one Dryden had shot in the cave. All that was left of its head was a few teeth attached to a scrap of chin. The ghoul coming through the window was the faceless one Raisy had gutted. A grey loop of intestine snagged on the jagged window frame and dragged behind it like a grisly party streamer.

The headless ghoul stood in the doorway between the living room and the front hallway. It seemed to look briefly at Dryden (as much as anything headless can "look"), then started up the stairs.

"Chester!" Dryden called out. "You got company coming!" He turned his attention back to the other ghoul as it came toward him. He backed away, still searching for a weapon, and bumped into one of the dining-room chairs. He picked it up and brought it down on the ghoul's head. The chair shattered into half a dozen pieces. The ghoul advanced.

Dryden realized he was running out of options and pulled out the greenwood gun. He aimed, braced himself, and pulled the trigger. The sound it made was closer to a scream than a gunshot. The cry of a pissed-off banshee, Dryden thought. A blast of that same witchy green fire exploded from the barrel and struck the ghoul in the shoulder, tearing off most of it and leaving its left arm dangling by a scrap of rotting sinew.

Dryden clutched his chest and slumped back against the wall.

The ghoul reached out with its intact arm and grabbed the gun by the barrel. It tried to pull the weapon out of Dryden's hand, but he held on tight. The ghoul swung him around and knocked him into the dining room table. Dryden pulled the trigger again, wincing at the heart-rending pain, and the ghoul's hand evaporated in a conflagration of swampfire that momentarily filled the room with its brilliance.

The ghoul looked at the spot where its hand had been and swatted Dryden backward onto the table. It was on top of him in a flash, its mouth open and a waft of fetid air buffeting his face. Dryden gagged. It was the smell of old spices and crops left to rot in autumn fields. It was the smell of tombs.

Raisy appeared in the broken window and saw Dryden and the ghoul struggling on top of the dining room table. She glanced at the wooden chandelier above them and took out a throwing knife. She yelled at Dryden to get out of the way. He splayed his hands against the ghoul's chest, pushed it up like he was bench-pressing a barbell, and quickly rolled off the edge of the table. He landed painfully on his side and made himself keep rolling.

DEADSTOCK

Raisy threw the knife. It cut one of the two thick ropes that supported the chandelier, and it swung heavily to one side. A second later the other rope snapped and it fell on top of the ghoul. Stepping over the windowsill, she wished the candles had been lit.

The ghoul was entangled in the spokes of the chandelier, but it wasn't going to stay that way for long. Raisy drew a long, thin skewer and drove it through the ghoul's stomach, pinning it to the table like a butterfly on a piece of corkboard. The ghoul suddenly reached out and grabbed her wrist. Its head snapped forward at a questing angle. Raisy screamed.

Then Dryden was beside her swinging a lantern into the ghoul's scabrous face, splashing all three of them with oil. Dryden pulled Raisy away before they went up in flames. The ghoul wasn't so lucky.

The skewer kept it pinned to the table, and they watched while it writhed and twisted, flinging burning chunks of itself all around.

Their attention was suddenly pulled away by the muffled booming sound of Chester's shotgun.

They ran upstairs and across the second-floor landing to the door at the end of the hallway. It was locked. Dryden kicked it in and they went through together.

Chester Groom lay facedown on the floor. Dryden started toward him, then caught something out of the side of his eye and stopped.

The remaining ghoul was standing in the corner of the room, motionless as a cigar store Indian. Dryden started to raise his pistol, bracing himself for the wave of pain and nausea that would follow, then lowered it. Raisy nudged his shoulder, but he ignored her. Something was wrong here. Why did Chester lock the door *after* the ghoul had gotten inside?

Raisy nudged him again, and he reluctantly turned around.

Ian Rogers

The Groom girls were on the far side of the room. Hattie and Eudora were crouched next to the bed, forming a protective shield around Kit, who peeked out from between them with wide, panicky eyes.

Bonnie Groom stood in the center of the room. She was holding the shotgun. It was aimed at Dryden and Raisy.

Dryden looked back at Chester and saw something he had missed in his rush to get inside: A thin wisp of smoke rising from a shredded hole in the back of his chambray workshirt.

"Drop your weapons," Bonnie Groom said in cold voice, "or I'll drop you."

Dryden raised his empty hand in a placatory gesture. "Put down the gun, Bonnie." He glanced at the ghoul, but it still wasn't moving. "You're not thinking straight. You don't know what you're doing."

"I'm not crazy," Bonnie said. "I knew exactly what I was doing. I had it all planned out. Then my father went and asked for your help." She frowned. "I didn't expect that. I thought he was too proud to do something like that."

"Bonnie," Dryden said, "this ain't you. Something's messing with your head. The dish..."

"What do you know about it?" she snapped. "Nothing! I found it. It chose me. The more I uncover, the more powerful I become. That's how they reward loyalty." She stared down at her father's body. "Not like that sad old man. He runs us like he does his cattle. He dragged us out here to the middle of nowhere, all because he couldn't face people no more after Mother left." She shouted at him like he could still hear her. "That's why she left, you damn fool! You're weak and you always have been!"

Dryden shook his head uncomprehendingly. "But how could you do it, Bonnie? He's your father."

"You can do anything if you put your mind to it." She smiled broadly. "Or not."

62

Raisy said, "You're not psychic, are you?"

Dryden watched as Bonnie averted her gaze, almost shyly. "Mother said the best way to predict the future was to make it happen yourself."

"You're a black witch," Raisy declared. "The devil's whore."

"Sticks and stones," Bonnie said. "Sticks and stones."

"You killed Jessie, too, didn't you? Your own sister."

Bonnie nodded absently and her eyes took on a faraway look. "I put the snake in the water bucket. I watched her die from my bedroom window. I needed to see if I *could* do it. After that, gutting those prospectors was child's play. I got them in the night, while they were sleeping. Just another chore around the ranch." She giggled. "The dish brought 'em back, just like it told me it would, and I set them to work on the cattle." She looked down at her father's body again. "I wanted him to pay for every godforsaken day I've had to spend out here. One steer at a time, just so I could watch it eat away at him."

"You're calling something here with the dish, aren't you?" Dryden said.

Bonnie shook her head. "No, I'm calling them *back*. They was here long before our father dragged us out here. Long before any of us was here."

"What are they?" Raisy asked.

Bonnie tittered and gripped the shotgun tighter. "You'll see. Now, put down that devil gun, cowboy."

"You're one to talk about devils, you witch."

Bonnie smiled condescendingly at him. "You silly pathetic man."

Dryden dropped his gun on the floor. It was still hot to the touch, and the number on the grip had changed to 11.

"Now," Bonnie said, "tell your harpy to lose her coat of knives." She shook her head disapprovingly. "So unladylike."

"So's killing your father," Raisy said.

Bonnie's face congested into a tight little ball of hatred. "You're just as bad as the cowboy. You don't understand anything. You don't know the difference between a killin' and a sacrifice."

"Honey, I hope I never do."

"There's a difference," she said vehemently.

"Not to your daddy," Raisy replied coolly.

"*Take it off.*"

"As you wish."

Raisy moved slowly, slipping out of one sleeve, then the other. Lowering her coat to the floor, she smoothly palmed the six-inch dart she kept in a pocket inside the left cuff.

"Now take off the satchel," Bonnie said.

The satchel hung across Raisy's chest. She pulled the strap up over her head and placed it carefully on the floor, flipping the top open.

"Whatcha got in there?" Bonnie said, leaning down. "More knives?"

"Not quite," Raisy said. Still crouched down, she let out a low hiss that was identical to the sound an angry cat would make.

A shape leaped out of the satchel and into Bonnie Groom's face. It was August Finch. He yowled as he went scrambling overtop of Bonnie's head.

Bonnie let out a frightened cry and jerked the shotgun around at the cat. Then she realized her error and swung the shotgun back at Raisy. She caught a glimmer of something in the air and then she was choking. She dropped the shotgun and clutched at the dart embedded in her throat. Blood seeped from the wound and greased her fingers, preventing her from pulling it out. She made a low gurgling sound that turned to a high, whistling gasp. Then Bonnie's hands fell to her sides and she pitched forward onto the floor.

A second later, the ghoul in the corner did the same.

Ian Rogers

13

THE next morning, they burned the ghouls in the yard and buried Chester and Bonnie Groom in the garden. Then Raisy took the girls to Ashes to purchase some items for their trip. There was an uncle in San Francisco, and the change in scenery would do the girls good.

Dryden stayed behind to begin the work of closing down the ranch. He packed the girls' clothes and belongings into a couple of steamer trunks and hauled them downstairs.

While he was pressing his hands into the small of his back and cursing himself for not waiting for Raisy to come back and help him, Dryden heard a board creak out on the porch. He drew the greenwood gun and crept over to the splintered remains of the front door.

The marshal, Tad Jacobs, was sitting in a rocker with his feet up on the porch railing. He turned and peered at Dryden from beneath the brim of his flat-crowned hat, then lowered his gaze to the greenwood gun.

"Thought you said it don't shoot right."

Dryden was confused for a moment, then he remembered what he had told Jacobs about the gun on the day they met. "Instinct," he said, holstering the gun. "Can't help it."

"I get that," Jacobs said. "A man can't help what he is."

The old man turned his head and looked out across the yard. The remains of the ghouls were smoldering in a pile in front of the corral. Dryden reminded himself he still had to spread the ashes once the fire burned itself out.

"Looks like you caught your man." Jacobs leaned forward, squinting his ancient eyes. "Or men, it looks like."

"Or neither," Dryden said. "No thanks to you."

"I came out and looked at the mutilations," Jacobs said, still staring straight ahead. "I did my part."

"You didn't do a damn thing," Dryden said. He could feel the anger boiling up inside him. "You just sat back and watched while it all happened."

"That's what we have to do sometimes," Jacobs said. "We watch. Some of us — a cynical few, I guess you could call 'em — say that's what we do best."

"I'm inclined to agree with them," Dryden said. "And who's 'us'? The marshals?"

Jacobs shrugged. "Close enough."

"People are dead here, Jacobs. People I cared about."

"It happens. It happened before and it'll happen again. Some of us stand by and watch it happen. Others try and stop it. I do what I do best. Can you say the same?"

Jacobs finally turned and looked at Dryden. There was a look of deep sadness in his eyes, and Dryden felt his anger dwindling like the fire in the yard.

Jacobs stood up, knees and back popping, and walked down the porch steps to where his horse was tied at the hitching rail.

"I'm sorry I missed your pretty redheaded friend. She's a looker, ain't she?"

Dryden didn't say anything.

"It's funny," Jacobs went on. "I recall hearing about a young lady who traveled with the Seaway-Twister Carnival. Nasty bit of business that group. Anyway, they say this lady was the best damn knife-thrower in the country. Maybe the whole world. I never seen her myself, and I heard she ain't with the carnival anymore, but you know the funny part? I heard she was a redhead, too. How about that?"

Dryden still didn't say anything.

"Well, I guess I should be on my way." Jacobs patted the side of his horse but made no move to mount up. "I guess you'll be heading out soon, too." He hesitated. "You mind if I give you a piece of advice?"

"Why not," Dryden said truculently. "You haven't given me anything else."

Jacobs ignored the jab. "You still got a problem, son. Out at that lakebed. You should deal with it before you go."

With that, Jacobs tapped the brim of his hat, climbed onto his mount, and rode away.

Dryden watched the marshal in black until he was only a dust cloud fading on the horizon.

Later that evening, Raisy and the girls came back with a small coach to carry them and their belongings, and a couple of strong buckskins that would take them to San Francisco.

That night, Dryden went out into the pasture alone. He took a dead rabbit with him.

He came back in the morning and told Raisy what they had to do.

Ian Rogers

14

DRYDEN scooped up a shovelful of dirt and dumped it on another exposed section of the dish.

"Tell me again why we're doing this?" Raisy asked him.

"Because it's what we need to do," Dryden replied.

"And why are *they* doing this?" She gestured at the Groom girls. Eudora and Hattie were working with garden hoes, while Kit was using a spade. August Finch stalked back and forth among them like a prison guard watching over a chain gang.

"They're helping," Dryden said. He didn't mention that the girls needed to do this as much as he did. They still weren't talking much, but he had seen a smile or two in the last few days. Letting them help bury the dish seemed to give them a sense of closure. Dryden didn't completely understand it, but there were plenty of things he didn't understand in this world. It was working, that's all that mattered, so he didn't question it.

Raisy, on the other hand, couldn't seem to stop questioning it.

"Shouldn't we be digging this thing up instead of covering it up?"

"Jacobs says the dish is our problem. Marmen says it isn't. I decided to split the difference and put it back the way it was."

"You talked to the marshal?" Raisy said. "When?"

"He came by the day you took the girls to town. We had a little chat. I think he knows something about us. And I'm almost positive he ain't no marshal."

Raisy stopped digging. "What does he know about us?"

"He didn't say. He just implied a few things." Dryden wiped sweat off his brow and leaned on his shovel. "He knew you used to throw knives in the carnival."

Raisy grunted. "That ain't much. I bet he doesn't know my first name."

Dryden looked at her for a long moment. "Hell, *I* don't know your first name." Raisy didn't say anything to that, and he continued to stare at her expectantly. "Well," he said, "what is it?"

Raisy said, "I'll never tell," and resumed digging.

Dryden shook his head and went over to see how the girls were doing. Eudora and Hattie were still hoeing, while Kit had taken off the bandanna she'd had wrapped around her head and was now covering it with dirt.

"Why are you doing that, peanut?"

"I'll never tell!" she burst out.

Hattie looked over at them and laughed. "I won't tell, either!"

"None of us will!" Eudora chimed in, and the girls — Raisy included — laughed.

Dryden stared at them for a moment, then shook his head again and went back to work.

ABOUT THE AUTHOR

IAN ROGERS is a writer, artist, and photographer. His short fiction has been published in *Cemetery Dance*, *Supernatural Tales*, and *On Spec*. He is the author of the Felix Renn series of supernatural-noir stories, including "Temporary Monsters" and "The Ash Angels."

Ian lives with his wife in Peterborough, Ontario. For more information, visit ianrogers.ca.

STONE BUNNY

WEIRD WEST